ZAHRA ♥

Zaki

♥

My Book of Pirates & Knights

W

FRANKLIN WATTS
LONDON · SYDNEY

CONTENTS

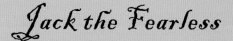

A Band of Dirty Pirates

by Damian Harvey

Illustrated by Graham Philpot

There was once a band of pirates

who sailed the seven seas:

a band of dirty pirates,
all with dirty knees.

They never washed their faces.

They never washed their hands.

Their fingernails were full of muck from digging in the sands.

Jolly Roger was their captain,
and the dirtiest one of all.

He hadn't had a proper bath
since he was very small.

After school, one summer's day,

he ran away to sea.

His mum had often wondered

just where her son could be.

Then one day she saw his ship

out sailing in the bay.

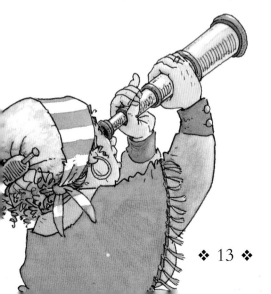

So she rowed out to say hello
before it sailed away.

Roger's mum was angry

when she saw the dirty bunch.

She made them walk the plank
for a wash before their lunch.

She made them rub and scrub

till they were squeaky clean.

Now they're the cleanest pirates
that the world has ever seen!

Sir Otto

by Mick Gowar

Illustrated by Martin Remphry

Sir Otto the Bold

was clever and strong.

His sword was sharp,

and his lance was long.

He could battle with giants

and dragons with wings ...

... three-headed monsters

and green, slimy things.

He could knock down
three knights with one
sweep of his lance.

He could play on the harp.

He could sing.

He could dance.

He was the best of all knights,

in body and brain.

But one day Sir Otto got

soaked in the rain.

His chainmail went stiff
and his joints set like glue.

In no time, his armour
was rusted right through.

He struggled to move,

with all of his might.

But the wet, rusty armour

held him in tight.

"Oh help me please someone!"

they heard Otto shout.

"I'm trapped in my armour!

I cannot get out!"

His wife, Lady Mary, cried,

"Hold on, my dear.

You need a tin-opener.

I've got one right here!"

So, turning the handle,

she undid his seams,

and opened him up
like a tin of baked beans!

Alfie
the
Sea Dog

by Mick Gowar

Illustrated by Mike Phillips

Alfie was a sea dog.

He sailed the seven seas.

He cooked the
sailors' breakfasts.

He made them cups of tea.

And when the sailors climbed
the ropes,

or raised the big

white sail ...

Alfie sang a jolly song
and wagged his jolly tail.

The sailors covered up their ears.

"Enough!" the captain roared.

"That really is an awful noise,

I beg you, please, no more!

Then one dark night,

far out at sea,

a new ship sailed along.

"More sailors!" Alfie thought. "Goodie!

I bet they'd like my song."

So Alfie threw his head back,

to sing with all his might.

The pirates all threw

down their swords,

and raised their

hands in fright.

"Don't hurt us!" screamed

the pirate chief.

"We give up!" shrieked

his crew.

"We've caught you now!"

the captain cried.

"It's off to jail for you!"

So Alfie was a hero and
he sang his song all day.

O OOOOOOO

The captain gave out earplugs ...

... and the sailors cheered,

HOOray!

OOOOOO

The Lonely Pirate

by Jillian Powell

Illustrated by Anna C. Leplar

There was once a lonely pirate.

He had no friends at sea.

He flew the Jolly Roger,

but no one was there to see.

It's easy to get lonely when there's nobody in sight –

just the blue sea and

the blue sky ...

...and the moon and stars at night.

Sometimes he played the fiddle,

but he made an awful din.

Sometimes he played Snap

on his own,

but then he'd always win.

Sometimes he climbed

the ship's mast,

to look for another boat.

Or he'd hook things

on his fishing rod,

to see if they would float!

He tried calling to the seagulls,
but they flew the other way.

He tried singing to the whales,

but he just scared them away!

Then one day he found an island,

with trees round a
mountain peak.

In the trees, he saw
a parrot with a red
and yellow beak.

He soon stopped being lonely once
he heard the parrot squawk.

For he took that parrot with him ...

...and he taught it how to talk!

Sir Talkalot
and the Dragon

by Sherryl Clark

Illustrated by Neil Chapman

Sir Talkalot was a brave knight

but he talked – a lot.

Every day he put people to sleep

with his long, boring stories.

One day, news came of a dragon

causing trouble in a far-off village.

The king sent Sir Talkalot to help.

When Sir Talkalot arrived,

he saw a terrible sight.

"What happened?" he asked.

"Did the dragon attack you?"

"No," said the mayor.

"The dragon can't get to sleep.
But he's so tired, he keeps
falling over," explained the mayor.

Sir Talkalot didn't want to kill the dragon just for being tired.

But something had to be done.

"I'll try talking to him," he said.

So Sir Talkalot climbed all the way

up to the dragon's cave.

The dragon looked very grumpy.

"Go away!" he growled.

Sir Talkalot drew his sword.

Then he had another idea.

"Let me tell you about the time
I won the Knight of the Year
Award," he said.

"Oh no!" groaned the dragon.

But Sir Talkalot began his tale.

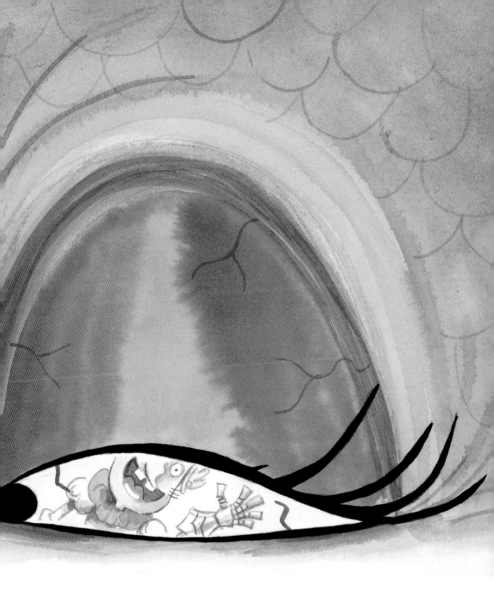

It went on ... and on ... and on.

The dragon closed his eyes.

When the dragon began
to snore, Sir Talkalot
had to stop.

The snore made his teeth rattle

so much that he couldn't talk!

The people in the village were
delighted. The only problem
was that now ...

… Sir Talkalot had yet another

tale to tell!

Pedro the Pirate

by Mick Gowar

Illustrated by Rory Walker

Pete was a pirate captain.

Most pirates are brave and fierce.

But Pete wasn't.

Pete's crew weren't brave or fierce either.
They got scared when the cannons
went bang.

They hid when the muskets
went crack.

Pete had a parrot called Pedro.

Pedro was brave and fierce.

❖ 134 ❖

He was also very clever.

He could say: "Pretty Pedro!" and "Pedro wants peanuts!"

Pedro listened carefully when the
cannons went bang and the muskets
went crack.

One morning, Pedro showed just

how clever he was:

"BANG! BANG! CRACK! CRACK!"

ANG!! BANG!!
CRACK!! CRACK!!

"Help!" shouted the pirates.

"We're being attacked!

What shall we do?"

"To the lifeboats!" cried Pete.

They got in the lifeboats and

started to row.

Then they saw who was making all
the noise. "Bother and blow,
it's Pedro!" said Pete.

"What shall we do now?"

asked the pirates.

"Row back to the ship!" cried Pete.

That night on the ship, Pete and his
pirates were woken up by loud noises.

BANG! went the cannons.

CRACK! went the muskets.

"What shall we do?" asked the pirates.

"Go back to sleep!" said Pete.

"It's only Pedro."

But it wasn't Pedro. It was
Bonecrusher Bill and his
fierce pirate gang!

The fierce pirate gang jumped
onto Pete's ship. "Tie their hands,
then make them walk the plank!"
cried Bonecrusher Bill.

Then Pedro had a good idea:

"BANG! BANG! CRACK! CRACK!"

"Help!" shouted the fierce pirate gang.

"We're being attacked!"

"Get back to our ship!" shouted

Bonecrusher Bill.

Pedro pecked the ropes. Pete and his

pirates were free!

"Three cheers for Pedro, our new pirate
captain!" shouted the crew.

Pirate Jack
and the
Inca Treasure

by Leslie Melville

Illustrated by Fabiano Fiorin

Once upon a time there lived a
sly pirate captain called Jack.

He and his crew sailed the seas
looking for treasure and
ships to steal.

But Captain Jack never wanted
to share any treasure with
the rest of his pirates.

One day, Jack's ship was sailing near
to Cocos Island.

He had a treasure map, and he
knew that there was a secret hoard
of treasure hidden deep in a cave
behind a waterfall.

People had told Jack that in the cave
there was gold, silver and a magical
sword that used to belong to Pachacuti,
a famous Inca warrior king.

Captain Jack thought of a plan
so that he could have the treasure
all to himself.

"We shall stop here, lads!" he yelled to
the rest of the pirates. "We need some
fresh drinking water."

Late that night, when Captain Jack thought everyone was asleep, he lowered a boat and rowed ashore. But he was being watched.

"I'll bet that scurvy dog is up to no good," said one of the pirates. "Let's follow him and find out," said the other.

Captain Jack landed on the island and made his way to the secret treasure cave.

He splashed through the waterfall and
squeezed into the hidden
cave entrance.

Glistening in the moonlight lay
Pachacuti's magical sword and many
other treasures.

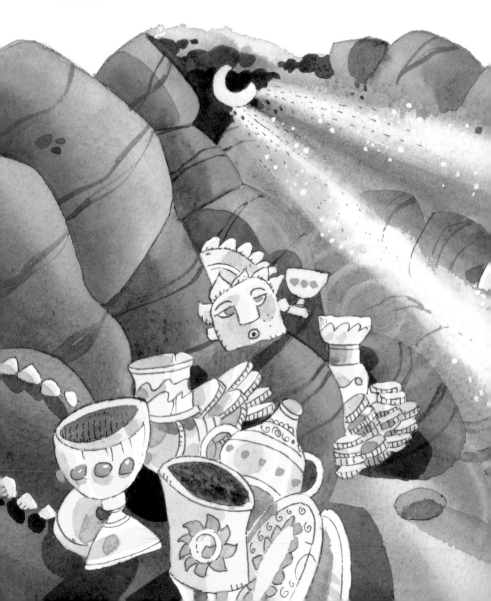

Jack put the sword in his belt, clutched some coins close to his chest and made his way out of the cave.

The two pirates who had followed him were waiting on the other side of the waterfall.

"Hello, Jack," said one. "We wondered where you were going."

"Seems as though we have some treasure to share," chuckled the other, "while you walk the plank!"

The pirates uncoiled a length of rope and took the coins from their captain. But they did not see the sword in their captain's belt.

Quick as a flash, Captain Jack raised the sword high in the air and cried out, "Pachacuti! Pachacuti! Pachacuti!"

In that moment, the two
pirates dropped the coins
and froze. Then, before
Jack's eyes, they both
turned to stone.

⊰ Pirate Jack and the Inca Treasure ⊱

Terrified by what he had seen, Captain
Jack picked up the coins and took
everything back to the treasure cave.
Then he raced
back to his ship.

The next morning, Jack sailed away.
He left two tall stones, that were
once cut-throat pirates, standing on
the island – and there they remain
to this very day!

Jack
the
Fearless

by Enid Richemont

Illustrated by Beccy Blake

Jack was a weaver, but he dreamed
of becoming a knight.

One day he painted his knight's
name on a saucepan lid:
Jack the Fearless.

Then he put the saucepan on his head
and picked up a stick.

He went to see his old donkey, Alfie,

who was busy eating carrots.

"I'm Jack the Fearless now," he cried.

"I've got a helmet, a shield and a sword. All I need is a horse."

"Eee-aaaw," sighed Alfie.

Jack decided to have an adventure.
He dragged Alfie away from
his carrots.

They plodded along the road until they
came to a castle.

The king was looking out of his
window. "Jack the Fearless,"
he read. "Just the man I need."

The king held a feast for Jack.

"Tomorrow," he declared, "you will fight

the great dragon."

Next morning, the king brought out
a splendid new saddle for Alfie.

Jack climbed slowly into the saddle.

He was already feeling scared.

The king whispered into Alfie's ear:
"Carrots forever if you've
fought the dragon by tea time."

And suddenly Alfie was off,
galloping like the wind.

After a while, Jack smelt a terrible
smell. He saw people running.
"Turn back!" they yelled.
"The great dragon's coming!"

"Stop, Alfie!" Jack cried. He tried pulling on the reins, but Alfie wouldn't stop.

Jack grabbed a tree branch.

"I'll be safe up here," he thought as Alfie galloped away.

Below, the dragon
started sniffing.
"I smell a man!"
she hissed.

Then she yawned. "But I've
already eaten twenty children,
so I can wait for my pudding."

The dragon closed her eyes
and started to snore.

❖ 200 ❖

"Now's my chance," thought Jack, and he began to scramble down. CRACK! A branch snapped, and he fell astride the dragon's neck.

The dragon woke up. "My pudding!" she roared. She turned her head to bite him, but Jack grabbed her horns.

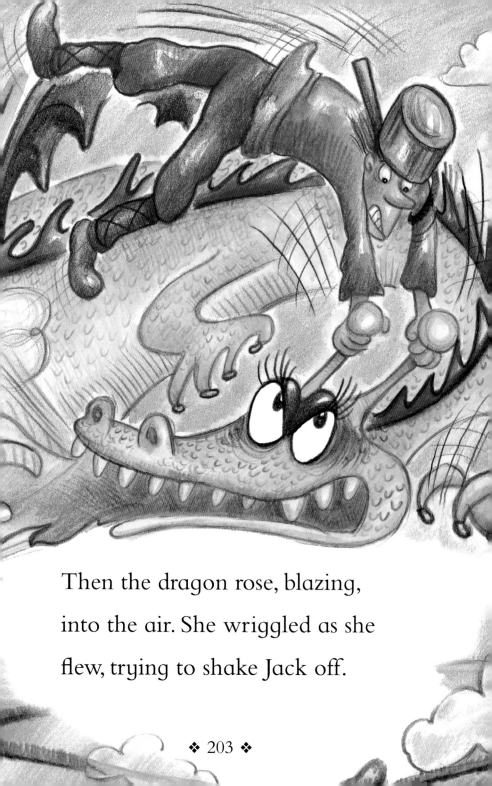

Then the dragon rose, blazing,
into the air. She wriggled as she
flew, trying to shake Jack off.

She was still wriggling when she flew
SPLAT! into the castle walls.

Jack was thrown from her neck, and landed back onto Alfie.

"You've killed the dragon!" cried the king. He was delighted. He gave Jack a castle, and Alfie his very own field of carrots.

And Sir Jack the Fearless and Lord Alfie
Carrot lived happily ever after.

Blackbeard the Pirate

by Mick Gowar

Illustrated by Mike Phillips

My name is John. When I was a small boy I fought the fiercest pirate in the world! This is my story.

It was a hot summer day. I was fishing
for crabs in the harbour of Sark island.
I looked out to sea.

A ship was in the distance. It had
black sails and a black flag with
white bones and
a skull. Pirates!

The pirates rowed ashore. Their
captain had burning fuses in his hair.
He looked like a devil! "My name is
Blackbeard," he shouted. "I am the
lord of this island now."

The pirates forced all the people to
bring their money and jewels to the
churchyard.

Blackbeard took everything and
locked everyone in the church.

But I was so small that nobody noticed me.

No one saw me climb into my little boat and sail away.

I sailed to the next island.

There was a warship

in the harbour.

"There are pirates on the Isle of Sark,"
I told the captain. "Please help us."
"How?" asked the captain.
"I have a plan," I said.

Next day we sailed into Sark
harbour. The captain and I
rowed ashore.

Blackbeard met us. "I am the lord of Sark," he said. "What do you want?"

"This boy's father was a passenger on my ship," the captain said.
"He died. May we come ashore to bury him?"

"Yes," said Blackbeard, looking at the
fine warship he hoped to steal.
"But first, you must give me all your
guns and swords."

Some of the captain's sailors rowed ashore with a coffin. Slowly we climbed the hill to the church.

All the people of Sark were inside. We closed the church doors.

The captain opened the coffin –
it was filled with guns and swords.

"Now we'll get those pirates,"
said the mayor. "Follow me!"

Some of the pirates tried to steal
the warship. But the captain had
set a trap.

The mayor and the islanders captured
the other pirates and locked them in
the church.

"I'll take these pirates to London," said the captain. "They will be put in prison."

No one saw Blackbeard climb into my little boat and sail away – except me. And no one noticed me because I was so small.

Now I am old, but I still look out to sea every morning and evening to make sure no ship with black sails and a black flag is sailing into the harbour.

❖ 229 ❖

Pirates
of the
Storm

by Enid Richemont

Illustrated by Andy Hammond

Long ago, there lived two women called
Mary Read and Anne Bonny.

Mary grew up in England. In those days, girls in England weren't allowed adventures. So Mary dressed up as a boy and ran away.

Anne grew up across the ocean in America. Like Mary, Anne longed for adventure ...

... so she married a pirate called Calico Jack.

One day, Mary arrived at a port.
"A life at sea looks exciting,"
she thought.

"Anyone need a cabin boy?"

Mary yelled.

A cruel captain grabbed her.

"I do," he growled.

Anne, too, longed to go to sea. But
Calico Jack's crew did not want her
on their ship. "Women bring bad luck,"
they growled.

Anne did not give up. One day, she

hid her hair and put on breeches.

"I'm your cabin boy now,"

she told Jack.

Meanwhile, Mary was having a very hard time on her ship. The cruel captain made her work day and night.

"Any slacking, boy, and I'll flog you!"

he snarled, cracking his whip.

After a few weeks, Mary's ship
sailed into the warm Caribbean
Sea. Anne and the pirates were
there, too.

"Wake up! Ship ahoy!" yelled Anne.
Jack rubbed his eyes. Then he
raised the skull and crossbones.
"Attack!" he cried.

Mary's ship fired its guns, but missed.

When the pirates clambered
on board Mary's ship, the captain
locked himself in his cabin.
"Fight, you cowards!" he yelled.

Mary grabbed a cutlass.

"I'll fight!" she cried.

Anne laughed.

"Come on then, cabin boy!"

But Mary fought hard.

"Truce!" gasped Anne.

"Agreed," cried Mary,

"if you take me with you."

The pirates loaded the captain's treasure chests onto their ship.

Mary went with them.

The crew opened the chests. They
found heaps of gold and jewels.
Jack opened a bottle of rum.
"Let's celebrate!" he yelled.

No one noticed that a mighty storm
was brewing until ...

… huge waves rocked the ship and
rain battered the sails.

The pirates grabbed Anne.

"We know you're a woman," they cried.

"This storm's all your fault!"

"Throw her overboard and get rid of the

bad luck," someone yelled.

Suddenly Mary leapt out, waving her cutlass. "I'm a woman too!" she cried. "And it's lucky we are here to sail this ship because you're all too drunk to do it!"

When Calico Jack woke up, Anne
and Mary were sailing into port.
"Hurrah!" yelled Mary.
"Let's work together," cried Anne. "We'll
be the best pirates in the Caribbean."

And for a while, they were!

First published in 2014 by
Franklin Watts
338 Euston Road
London NW1 3BH

Franklin Watts Australia
Level 17/207 Kent Street
Sydney NSW 2000

The author and illustrator acknowledgements on
pages 4, 24, 48, 74, 102, 130, 156, 182, 208, 230 consititute
an extension of this copyright page.

A CIP catalogue record for this book is available
from the British Library.

ISBN 978 1 4451 2738 5

Editor: Jackie Hamley
Designer: Chris Fraser
Cover designer: Cathryn Gilbert

Printed in China

Franklin Watts is a division of Hachette Children's Books,
an Hachette UK company.
www.hachette.co.uk